PERCY AND THE FIVE HOUSES

by Else Holmelund Minarik

pictures by James Stevenson

Puffin Books

PUFFIN BOOKS
Published by the Penguin Group
Viking Penguin, a division of Penguin Books USA Inc.,
375 Hudson Street, New York, New York 10014, U.S.A.
Penguin Books Ltd, 27 Wrights Lane, London W8 5TZ, England
Penguin Books Australia Ltd, Ringwood, Victoria, Australia
Penguin Books Canada Ltd, 2801 John Street, Markham, Ontario, Canada L3R 1B4
Penguin Books (N.Z.) Ltd, 182–190 Wairau Road, Auckland 10, New Zealand

Penguin Books Ltd, Registered Offices: Harmondsworth, Middlesex, England

First published in the United States of America by Greenwillow Books,
a division of William Morrow and Company, Inc. 1989
Reprinted by arrangement with William Morrow and Company, Inc.
Published in Picture Puffins 1990
1   3   5   7   9   10   8   6   4   2
Text copyright © Else Minarik Bigart, 1989
Illustrations copyright © James Stevenson, 1989
All rights reserved

LIBRARY OF CONGRESS CATALOGING IN PUBLICATION DATA
Minarik, Else Holmelund.
Percy and the five houses / by Else Holmelund Minarik;
pictures by James Stevenson.   p.   cm.
Summary: None of the five different houses Percy receives from the
House of the Month Club proves to be as perfect as his own beaver home.
ISBN 0-14-054209-4 : S3.95
[1. Dwellings–Fiction.   2. Beavers—Fiction.]   I. Stevenson,
James, 1929–   ill.   II. Title.
PZ7.M652Pe   1990   [E]—dc20   90-8230

Printed in Hong Kong
Set in ITC Bookman

FOR BOB AND KAS BENDINER,

FOUNDERS

OF THE

HOUSE

OF THE

MONTH

CLUB

It was a fine day in July.

Percy played by the river.

There he found some gold.

"Why—that's real gold!" said Grandpa.

Lucky Percy.

He was rich!

Along came Ferd the fox.

"I am rich," said Percy to Ferd.

"See my gold."

"My, my!" said Ferd. "So you are,
Percy. Now you can belong to
The House of the Month Club."

"If you give me the gold," said Ferd,
"I can put your name on this card,
like this:

HOUSE OF THE MONTH
CLUB

PERCY

Then you will belong to the club."

"What is The House of the Month Club?"
Percy wanted to know.
"The House of the Month Club is a club
that sends you a house a month,"
said Ferd. "You will have
an August house, a September house,
an October house, a November house,
and a December house."

"I like that," said Percy.

"Here is the gold, Ferd."

"And here is your card, Percy,"
said Ferd. "Now you belong to the
club. You are a lucky beaver!"

In August the first house came.

It came in a big box.

It was a cardboard house.

Grandpa and Percy took it out

and put it all together.

What a fancy house!

Percy ran to call the family.

They all came to see the new house.

There it was, up in a tree.

"The wind took it," said Grandpa.

That was too bad.

But the birds liked it.

In September a second house came.

Grandpa and Percy put it together.

It was a castle—

a real cardboard castle!

Percy and his friends played in it

—and on it

—and all through it.

And then it rained.

Soon there was no more castle.

"I can't wait for October,"

said Percy.

In October a third house came.

It came in a small package.

What could be in that small package?

Why—it was a teepee!

It was a beautiful Indian teepee,

all made of crepe paper.

Now wasn't that fun!

Too bad, the fun did not last long.

Soon the teepee was gone.

Everyone had a little bit of it.

What would come in November?

Percy could not wait for November.

In November another small package came.
And in it was a dear little camper.
Grandpa put the wheels on it.

"But it is too small!" said Percy.

"Not for us," said some mice.

They pulled it away.

And that was that.

"What next?" said Grandpa to Percy.

It was growing cold.
It was icy and snowy.
And then in December a truck
pulled up. Ferd got out and
unloaded the truck.

"Look here, Percy," he said.

"This is your last house.

How do you like it?"

"An igloo!" cried Percy.

"My goodness!" said Grandpa.

"We don't need it!" said Mother.
"We don't need one more house!
 We have one, you know, out there
 in the water.
 It won't blow away.
 It won't fall down.
 It won't tear,
 and we can all fit into it.
 So come along, you two. Winter is here,
 and everyone is waiting for you."

"Well, Ferd," said Percy.

"You can have the igloo."

"Why—thank you," said Ferd.

"I will vacation at the North Pole."

Percy and Ferd loaded the igloo
back into the truck.

"I'm off," said Ferd.

He waved to Percy.

Percy waved back.

Soon Ferd was out of sight.

Percy slid down into the water.

He swam out slowly.

He made a wide circle.

He ducked under.

Then he was home.

"I know something," said Percy to the family.

"I know that this little house is the best
house for beavers."

"Percy," said Grandpa, "you are absolutely right!
This is the best little house for us!"